Angels of Death

The Gifted, Volume 2

Londa Cele

Published by Londa Cele, 2023.

ANGELS OF DEATH

First edition. May 27, 2023.

Copyright © 2023 Londa Cele.

ISBN: 979-8223937104

Written by Londa Cele.

Also by Londa Cele

The Gifted
Someone New
Angels of Death

Unsupervised
Questionable Decisions

Standalone
Nomalungelo
Wedding Vows
Thando's Strength

Watch for more at www.londacelenovelz.wordpress.com.

Angels of Death

1

Dube's Church of True Believers, or DCTB for short, was one of the biggest churches in the city if not the biggest, having one of the most renowned messengers from God to preach his message. Pastor Dube or Asanda Dube, as his ID book would know him was a Pastor like none other. While others did the standard practice of laying hands on members of the church and praying for their well-being, you know, elementary things. Dube, on the other hand, was a true miracle worker, bringing back cell phones with no battery to full charge, women with period pains to suffer no more, making it rain money and the list goes on. One of the best perks of attending the DCTB was it was one of the first digitally advanced churches around. Sure, you had to pay a subscription fee, but that's usually the case with innovation. On the flip side, tithing was optional and boy did his devotees make use of this option. Besides Dube's miracles, what made him such a prominent figure was the fact that an old woman once tithed with a large portion of her pension and in return, he bought her a house. Fully paid, fully furnished and the best part of it all, she no longer lived in the township. How true that story was between Dube, the old lady and God. If it happened in the first place.

Dube was an animated preacher, making falling asleep during one of his sermons virtually impossible, both in the figurative and literal sense. Giving a chance for the new and unfamiliar to catch their breath and on the other side of the eBible, a chance to subscribe. Simply put, it was an extravaganza and this Sunday was no different, with a stage filled with two men and a nurse behind him as he continued to preach.

"Bazalwane (My faithful worshipers), what I have here, in this bottle is a sample of sperm, freshly prepared this morning and most importantly blessed by the Lord," he said, raising it as high as he could to show his entire congregation. "And with this blessing, I will take it upon myself to do the Lord's work and gift an unfortunate, misfortuned and ill-fated soul a blessing. Let whoever shall emerge from this be known as Cain, Abel, Seth and so forth. Can I get an Amen!"

"Amen!" the church shouted.

"For all those who still doubt God's power for whatever reason, I bring forth to you Doctor Ntando Ntombela. A specialist in reproductive endocrinology, simply put, a specialist doctor that deals in fertility."

The man waved timidly as the church welcomed him with a concert-like entrance before being asked a few questions and being asked to verify the bottle of semen in front of the hundreds of eyes watching in the church and thousands more online while Dube found an individual to bestow this magnificent gift with. Ignoring the cheers and shouts from those who wanted it, wanted his touch and fainted at his presence being so close to him.

"Ma'am, could you please come with me?" he said, uttering softly into his microphone as he stretched out his hand.

She etched herself towards him, squeezing past other congregants toward his open palm before being pulled back.

"Woah, relax!" her brother ordered.

"Sir, it's fine. It's what the Lord wants,"

"Chief, the Lord can wait. Mandisa, where do you think you're going?" he asked.

"Relax, this stuff is fake anyway," she said, snatching her arm away from him and grabbing Dube's awaiting palm.

"True believers, faith and belief have led me to believe this woman's name is Mandisa, is this true?"

Mandisa nodded, rolling her eyes.

"Amen," the church echoed, with a few claps of disbelief in between.

"Miss, or shall I say Mandisa, if you could please follow me," he said as he led her back to the centre of the stage.

With the five of them on the stage, Dube explained how he, through the power of the Lord, was going to make Mandisa pregnant using nothing but blessed sperm checked by a specialist. Seemed easy enough and with that explanation, the nurse, a witness, a specialist and Mandisa were off to do the Lord's work and perform a miracle.

Moments Later

The ensemble returned in the exact manner in which they had disappeared. Mandisa's disappearance only done to preserve her dignity. Pastor Dube announced the success of his miracle and the church went ballistic. Mandisa's presence on the stage was highlighted online and by the zoom function on some congregants' photos. Her brief stint in the limelight ended with her being escorted off the stage, and those who had not been initially chosen to be part of the show were clearly displeased, showing their discontent. However, nobody disapproved more than her own family, particularly her brothers and none more so than Given.

The ride home was awkward and quiet, despite Joyce listening to a list of her favourite songs from Pastor Dube's catalogue of music. Given couldn't stop looking at her younger sister through the rear view mirror and avoided crashing on two occasions while she spent the entire ride home staring out the window. Given's sour mood would pass, they expected a grown man to act like a Sunday school child but his resilience was starting to make it uncomfortable to be around.

"Ma," Emmanuel interrupted, the disruption to her phone call intentional.

"It's Given. We can't live like this anymore, please talk to him, he's still upset about what happened at church last week and it's chased Mandisa away,"

"To where?"

"That's the thing, we don't know,"

<h1 style="text-align:center">2</h1>

When Joyce arrived in the living room, the mood was expectedly tense and her children reminded her of how they used to act back when they were young and had disputes they couldn't resolve on their own. Given their age, it was both cute and disappointing to see that they couldn't resolve it on their own, but thank God there were no women to suffer through their bickering.

"Ayi, friend, I'll have to call you back. As old as the men in this house are, they still act like children," Joyce sighed, ending her call on the phone and following her son to her living room. "Can somebody explain to me what's going on and why you're acting like your father?" Pointing at Given. "He didn't turn me into a single mother because it was the right thing to do and I didn't raise any of you to follow in his footsteps, let alone practise his actions on your own sister,"

After a round of silence, Emmanuel drew up the courage to speak, "Given and Mandisa fought about what happened at church. When they fought, he called her a whore, she left and we don't know where she is because she left her phone," he said, swinging it in his hands.

"Given," Joyce said, looking at her son.

Given sat with his arms crossed over his legs on the couch.

"The fact that you're 30-something years is an impressive achievement but I will not beg you to speak to me, especially in my house," Picking up the nearest decorative ornament that was nearest to her. "If you want to leave like your sister, be my guest. But know that's where you'll stay because there's no man of the house in this house but me. I serve tea to no one,"

"Emmanuel doesn't know what he's talking about," he coughed, "That's not true. Mandisa left after I kept asking her what happened at

5

church. When she left and when she returned she was two completely different people. She was angry and disappeared,"

Even though Given despised the man, a part of him hoped that Pastor Dube would be the miracle worker to bring back his sister, even though he didn't believe in his miracles. She didn't pitch to church and when he or his brothers tried to approach Dube, his entourage of thugs made quick work of pinning them against whatever surface they could to keep them as far away as possible from him. This... undoubtedly meant, Dube recognised them, he just wanted nothing to do with them. That or he was a pastor who wanted to stay the hell away from people unless he was performing miracles, but when Joyce tried to talk to him, she could slither past the wall of muscle. Talking to the man himself, however, proved to be another challenge as he denied her existence, claiming he performed miracles on many people, her face not even ringing a bell even when provided with photographic evidence.

The week that followed revealed nothing of Dube's unfamiliar miracle by-product, nor did the weeks that followed after that until enough days had passed to report Mandisa missing to the police. All that was left now was for them to do their job, prayer and have faith in the lord. Faith, a cruel untangible word imbued with effects heavily felt, its definition placing the strength of the Baloyi's shoulders on display as the only daughter out of three started to gain attention. As the saying goes, everything bad that happens also has a good way of looking at it. In Emmanuel's point of view, it meant that his sister's disappearance was finally getting some attention; however, on the flip side, it meant being the talk of the town in order for it to happen, something his family didn't appreciate. It was something that didn't make sense either given how much his mother loved to gossip about other people and basically how she spent her free time but who was he to judge? Joyce hated the attention, her phone was always busy, she felt like a call centre worker, always answering the same questions and even some she didn't know the answers to or darn right didn't want to know about Mandisa.

People seemed to forget she wasn't the reason she was missing in the first place but the person they avoided asking these stupid questions in the first place.

Mandisa's disappearance was ill-fated but its attention brought light to conversations that were hardly ever spoken in society, let alone in the church community. But if there was somebody who could help other than divinity itself it was somebody to whom divinity could speak through. Dube's Church of True Believers would live up to its name even if the person it was named after felt a particular way with the attention and ultimately his source of income being diverted somewhere else. Given sat in the lounge trying to ignore his mother and the fact that she was streaming her DCTB sermon, his mind too busy preoccupied with stacks of information and countless what-if possibilities filled by the lead investigator on Mandisa's case from the police. Until the following reunited him with reality.

"Blessed members of the church, to hear what has happened to one of our own members of this fine and magnificent church brings nothing but pain and misery," Pastor Dube sighed. "But nothing is impossible without, patience, perseverance and prayer. Can I get an amen?"

His mother listened, obeying the instruction while he sat there quietly trying to figure out what he'd done to or at the very least would do to his sister's name if he actually had nothing to do with her disappearance. One thing they both knew with certainty was it wasn't prayer as he continued to stream the sermon along with his mother.

"Satan has enjoyed himself for too long without consequences and as a messenger and tool of the almighty I have been commissioned to do something about it in order to stop his people from unhindered tyranny,"

A cheer rang through the church before the pastor eventually calmed them down, preparing them for the next set of words to leave his mouth. "I have been chosen by God to do what no man has done before, to walk the same path Noah did when he was told to build the Ark when Moses was told to part the sea in two. I Asanda, will find the missing child known as Mandisa Baloyi and return her to this very stand to fulfil the cavity the mere mention of her name exhumes," he pointed.

Hordes of members' cheers and screams rang through the church, overpowering those of non-believers and fainters of disbelief before Asanda forced his church into an unprepared ending with prayer. His actions ruffled a few feathers with his declaration of doing what taxpayer's money was paid to do, merely because he'd given them enough time and they'd failed and now it was his turn to show them how it was done.

3

Given had given up hope in looking for his sister, making him the last of the Baloyi's searching for Mandisa to do so. Letting go was enough motivation to allow the police to divert the same resources onto somebody else. The fact that he had to declare her missing and officially and come to terms with the fact that his sister was lost, gone or God forbid dead and had a hand to play in it and it ate at him in a way nobody could understand. Even if his sister's disappearance was what the universe had intended, all he wanted was an opportunity to apologise and then let it take its course. He'd have to live with the brunt of being blamed for her disappearance for the rest of his life, a part of him was ready to take on that responsibility but another was prepared to tell them to fuck off.

However, everybody linked to Mandisa was true to their word, even Asanda's brother, Sakhile, who kept far from any spotlight, pulled in his fair share of the weight and helped to look for the woman of the moment. But as a Dube, he stuck to what he did best and was most renowned for within the praise and worship community. Spearheading the movements of his brother's financial endeavours. A man who valued money before love, women and one who, perhaps before the eyes of God, whose first love was greed, given the success of DCTB.

Even though the bible had seven deadly sins within them, one could make a compelling case he was immune to six and it would hold water. Unlike his brother who was the face of Christianity, it was the lack of perfection that made Asanda... great. Another sermon was at full capacity and a record amount of views streaming online, but for the first time in a long while, if he was honest with himself, Sakhile was feeling nervous. What made things even worse was the fact that he couldn't pinpoint why? Change often spurred such feelings, but at the same time, a useless excuse to use given how much change he'd instilled in all the people on the other side of the curtain. Both from those seeking it and those who didn't know they needed it. He approached the stage and took a couple of deep breaths, a flood of old memories cheering him on in a way a boxer could relate to.

"Members of the church please help me in welcoming Sakhile Dube, a member of this family and my own and one whom none of what we have here would be possible without his ingenuity," Asanda pointed, catching his brother off-guard while on his phone.

He shook his head, moving the drone, filming him away from his face before succumbing to the hall chanting his name. Shaking his head in disappointment emerged from the protection of backstage to join his brother in the spotlight and ignored the cheering in the process. "How the hell did this man put up with all this noise," he thought to himself as they exchanged introductions as if there wasn't anybody seated in the stadium who didn't know that he was Asanda's older brother.

"Mr Dube, please tell us what brings you to the stage?" Asanda asked.

"Well Pastor," he said, rolling his eyes. "I come bearing good news. All our prayers have not been in vain. For the last time, I was amongst such a loyal crowd towards the Almighty we were able to gift that soul as a church with a child,"

"Amen," Asanda shouted, waving his arms.

"It is with that same joy and amazement that I want to bless myself with such presence,"

"Meaning?"

"Saying it won't do the power of this miracle any justice and as the saying goes, seeing is believing and nobody believes more and better than those united by the Dube Church of True Believers,"

"I still don't understand what you mean Sakhile,"

"Ladies and gentlemen of the church, saints and sinners, please would you put your hands together in helping me welcome Mandisa Baloyi," pointing to the wall behind him.

Security had to work overtime, trying to keep those with cameras unable to get clear footage of what they had just heard from being denied a chance to get proper footage. All in an effort to avoid their videos or pictures being called fake or worse... photoshopped. True to Sakhile's words, Mandisa appeared, like a salad on a plate during festivities. She was the last thing to appear on stage. Her appearance meant different things to many people, but Asanda found it impossible to hide the smile on his face as he watched the servers, unable to handle the amount of traffic from the people on the net. The tears from some of his most devoted believers at his most powerful miracle yet and the buckling of knees from their pastor, illustrating the power and strength it took from him. Yet, three pairs of eyes that watched in silence as Sakhile Dube slung his arm around Mandisa's shoulder, wrapping her around him as she tried to avert her face from drones that wanted unhindered and exposed shots of her face and more importantly, an initial reaction of being back from nowhere.

"Can I get a Hallelujah?" Asanda shouted at his church.

"Hallelujah!!" The stadium vibrated.

"Amen, amen, amen,"

"Amen!" the church repeated.

"Amen, a man. In whose man we trust?" he said, throwing his hands in the air.

"Dube!"

"Sorry guys, Miss Baloyi would like some time to lie down, she's been through a rough ordeal. She'll answer questions later once she's managed to gather enough strength, thank you for understanding," the brothers rehearsed as they ushered Mandisa away backstage.

"Is that really her or a look-alike?" Emmanuel asked, breaking the silence in the house.

"Oh, God, my poor child," Joyce sniffed, a stray hand muffling the end of her words, wiping her face of any stray tears with a tissue.

"There's only one way to find out," Given said. His words soft, but loud enough for his brother to hear him on the other side of the three-seater couch between them, as he continued to stare at the tv.

"Plan?" Emmanuel asked.

"Ask Mandisa where she's been and tell her to come back," he said, standing up, ignoring the eyes that followed him, taking his mother's leftover tea and accessories to the kitchen.

4

Joyce wasn't an idiot nor did she appreciate being treated like one, that being said, all her children had a clear understanding that she was done dealing with the police. Her job with them regarding missing persons and Mandisa was over a long time ago. Her sudden reappearance and their re-interest in her case weren't about to change that. They would have to find another way to do their job and identify bodies on their own. With such encouragement from their mother, one would assume that's what her duo of boys would follow in her footsteps and give law enforcement the finger, but it seemed not everybody in the Baloyi clan felt the same about the men in blue. On their way to church, the reality of the situation regarding their daughter and the DCTB soon dawned on them, calls for assistance in trying to find their missing family member went unanswered.

For a loud character on stage, he sure had mastered the art of being the opposite of it. It was to remain that way until God knows who, the next of kin? Or the silent Dube as they were jokingly known amongst the Baloyi's extended a much-needed helping hand of support. Information on Mandisa's whereabouts and well-being. When the family reached the church, they waited outside in the same way a boyfriend in a car would for their partner to emerge from the tyranny of what set them running towards the freedom of their car in the first place. Their car's unholy stance outside the holy building was discontinued by the emergence of the silent Dube to join them.

Their conversation was brief. The silent Dube leaned against the door much like a prostitute with a client, his purpose with the Baloyi's finished once they'd finished tailgating the black BMW he now found himself in. A fight broke out amongst the clan left behind, whether the number plate that read Dube 2-ZN was due to it being Asanda's second car or his brothers before being shut up as both cars pulled up to a local private hospital. The mood changed in both cars and as it elevated, it led them out of the lift. Scurrying through the hospital like rats, negligent of any help from medical staff, it was clear that this was not the first time Dube had been down these corridors.

A tap on the door and a show of their face and Mandisa's cheeks widened as though they were being pulled by someone from behind before being let go as she saw her brother storm past the Dube that was here to keep their word regarding her wellbeing.

"See for yourself. We've done nothing to her, she's fine," they pointed.

"Hey sis," Emmanuel winked.

"What the hell are you doing here?" Given demanded, shaking his sister.

"Hey, Given. Not here, not now. That's not how we practised it in the car, pull yourself together or go wait outside and wait for us to tell you what happened," Emmanuel said.

Given clicked his tongue before raising his head to acknowledge his sister and receiving one in return.

"Good to see you're safe, reliving the glory days, I mean, the last time you were in a place like this you were being born," Emmanuel smirked. "Coming home or still sightseeing?"

"I'll let you know," she laughed.

"And you?" turning to Dube. "You lost?"

"I believe the words you're looking for are thank you, but who's keeping track? Anyway, it was a pleasure, may the Lord bless you all and your endeavours," they finished, squeezing between the two men in the room.

"I want to come back home, please take me with you, I can't stay here. I know I fucked up, I couldn't come back because of Mom. Just take me with you, please,"

"Ma?" Given asked, confused.

"Okay, it's kinda late to discharge you now, but we'll be here first thing in the morning," Emmanuel said, confused.

"Morning is too far," Mandisa cried, holding onto her brother.

The two males looked at each other in confusion.

"Okay, don't worry, let me keep you some company and you can tell me what happened while Given looks for a nurse in order to do the paperwork. How's about that, at least it's a compromise?"

She nodded reluctantly while one of her brothers did what they were told and began looking for help. Watching her sister take her medication of some sort reminded Given too much of his mother's stints in hospital and had to watch in the safety of outside her room before finding himself doing something stupid like lashing out at an innocent nurse doing their job. With one problem down, it was now onto the next one, getting her discharged and finding out why she was in there in the first place and why she was so desperate to leave.

True to her family's word, Mandisa woke up with her luggage packed while her mental, physical and most importantly, emotional strength all returned to her. When they all arrived home, her mother smothered her in a hug that covered her chest in tears, not that she cared. After all she'd done, her family had literally welcomed her back with open arms as though she'd been unaccounted for due to work-related issues.

Soon things settled down and eventually, Mandisa would have to account for what had happened to her. Doing so was like peeling the shell off a boiled egg. Joyce pulled her children to the side while her daughter slept, everything they'd just heard was bullshit. She had a hunch, it had never left her astray; it was the same one that had confirmed Emmanuels' existence.

"What the hunch say, Ma?" Given grinned.

"Mandisa is pregnant," she said swiftly. Her children looked at her and began to argue, but none of them spoke up against their mother's statement.

"How?" Given asked.

"Sex, how else you idiot,"

"Keep talking shit like that and Mandisa won't be the only person in this family to be fetched from the hospital," Given pointed.

"But Ma-" Emmanuel began.

"She does nothing but sleep, vomit, pee and look at her, she looks like a balloon,"

"She might have been living the good life. After all, we fetched her at a private hospital, as for the other symptoms, they could be a coincidence," Given shrugged.

"Riiight,"

"Ma, warn him, it's going to happen," Given growled.

"Aga, you two grow up, you're both thirty, live in your mother's house and act like toddlers. Keep up this shit and the next thing Mandisa and I are picking are the cemetery to house you in," she said, clicking her tongue. "Your sister is pregnant. Now stop bickering and find out who's been fondling my poor baby and hasn't paid damages,"

Emmanuel was convinced his mother was talking shit until the smell of fish in the oven, something not even Given could burn, put his sister off. He watched her as she ran off to take care of her nausea before startling her when she finished, blocking her way back to the lounge and locking her in the bathroom.

"We need to talk," he whispered.

"What the hell are you doing? Emmanuel, I'm not in the mood for your games, let me go,"

"I've got fish outside, and it only makes one of us vomit, so start talking. How many months?"

Mandisa took offence before trying to get out of the toilet.

"Have it your way then," her brother sighed before he pulled out his secret weapon.

"Okay, okay, okay," she reeled back. "Close to four months,"

"Look at you," he smiled. "Ah, look at that, I'm going to be an uncle. So who's decided to hit and run?"

Mandisa rolled her eyes. "I can't remember, I was drunk. Maybe high, like I said, I can't remember,"

Her brother brought the fish closer.

"I'm being serious, I swear,"

"And Dube, what's the story with him?"

Mandisa fell silent, her eyes focused on the fish as it danced in her brother's hand. She ignored his threats as contemplated what was easier to bear, the truth or the constant vomiting.

"I can't say, they made me sign a non-disclosure in case anything happens,"

"So what, you honestly think I care? In the time you've been gone become one of his spies, or better still, wear a recorder? I'm not Given. I think using the head above my shoulders not the one above my knees, so please," he said, tapping the side of his head.

"Remember the miracle,"

"Yeah, why?"

"Well, the stuff in that bottle wasn't just milk and water," Mandisa said, pushing the fish away.

5

Mandisa forced her brother not to break his promise and tell anybody else. Truth be told, on any other occasion, he would've respected his sister's wishes, however, she was thinking out of fear and not a solid mind. That and it was too much to bear on his own. He confirmed the news with his mother whose response was rather anti-climactic, instead of the fireworks he expected her to eject; it was a mere "told you so,". That is as far as his news went, how it got to Given's ears was beyond him, but since he looked for a reaction with fireworks, his brother didn't spare any expense in giving him one. Once things died down and Given was convinced on multiple occasions not to confront his sister about the news, things returned to relative normalcy, with everybody even going back to church. But being at church never felt the same for anybody. Each member having their own reasons. After the service, the Baloyi's tried to talk to a Dube but were unsuccessful. With no luck, they waited outside the church for a week but still had no success. Just as Emmanuel had given up hope, his brother reminded him to stay positive. Moments later, a gold car with tinted windows exited the church's parking lot. A piece of paper stuck at the back reading Dube 7-ZN to rid any doubt and confirm that it was indeed the man they were waiting for. Their polo crept behind at an unsuspicious distance as it transitioned from urban sprawl to suburbia.

Seeing the man's estate, it was quite clear that it would be impossible to get into and so if they were to confront him, it would have to be before the end of his journey home. And so, on another unassuming day whereby the Dube's and Baloyi's paths happened to intersect with Given behind the wheel, all it took was an innocent nudge from behind that wouldn't be appreciated by insurance companies. The range stopped, its taillights glowed red and giving a sneak peek of what their driver looked like before they revealed themselves to find out who had dented his new car. Hyped up on adrenaline, it was a little too late when realising what was happening, his rush of testosterone evaporated as Given threw him to the ground, knee on chest and punched him while his brother waited for his turn. They beat the living shit out of him despite his cries and pleads that he didn't do it, nor was responsible for Mandisa's pregnancy through coughs of blood. A threat to kill him was enough to have his silence as he lay battered and bruised, leaking blood. The Baloyi's polo reversed before disappearing out of sight alongside his car with a dented rear bumper, injured and damaged just like him as they both lay on the street.

His car switched off and the sound of the car door echoed around him. The sound of feet could be heard scurrying around and he was more afraid of them confronting him than the other way around.

"Dad?"

"Mmm," he croaked.

There was silence and he knew it was due to fear more than it was shock. He watched her calling for help but managed to convince her to drive them home instead. Emergency services in South Africa weren't renowned for their efficiency and chances were he'd die waiting for them.

"You okay," he said, from the passenger seat as he lay there, reclined back.

"Yeah, I saw everything," she answered in a shaky voice.

"Everything?" he asked, confused.

"Yes,"

"How? You were in here like you were supposed to. Safe from those hooligans,"

"When you stopped you put the car in reverse and the reverse side camera came on and I watched what happened from there,"

They fell silent and let the radio fill in the awkward silence trying to fill in the giant space in the SUV.

"I recorded it so that the police can help me in case anything happened to you,"

"Well, would you look at that, don't worry baby, nothing will happen to me. Okay, when we get home, send this to your uncle while I get some rest okay,"

"Okay,"

Watching a WhatsApp video that wasn't the best quality through no fault of its own sent these churchgoers' emotions through the roof. Faith, if any, long gone, and a shame given that they ran an organisation entirely based on it. Watching the video repeatedly as though something had disturbed them the first time or out of sheer disbelief. The gnawing sensation of not being able to be of any help wouldn't stop. Torturing themselves for no reason with this video had no purpose, but anybody that had an inkling of involvement knew that anybody but their victim would use their head and not heart, from now on.

Asanda watched the video silently over a few drinks of alcohol older than he was.

"Want to talk about the video later, there's still something I can't get?" he said, his glass of whiskey in one hand and twirling his phone around in the other.

"Yeah sure, whatever. When I get back," Sakhile replied before juggling his attention between the phone beside his ear and the one in front of him. Sending a version of his own, the only bits of text that accompanied the footage was: *I thought we had a deal.*

"Do we have to do it like this, can't we do the sermon online? It's not like it's an impossible option,"

"You wanted to talk then let's talk. Shares have stagnated, membership is down 15% and tithes 18 if we round it up. The only thing that's made money thus far is the sale of eBibles and those toys of yours playing with water. I'm sorry but as much as you want it to happen, you can't copyright walking on water nor splitting it in two, trademarking is a different question,"

"What do you mean membership is down, these people come in here and fill up the stands like a leaking tap?"

"Two things. Oh, holy one. Not everybody who enter's those doors are old enough to tithe despite having their parents pay for them to come in. Once you can get an eight-year-old to pay and not get arrested for it, then I'm on board. Secondly, this miracle of yours is the root of our problems. Want a solution? Time to make like Noah, build a place to hide our assets and flood this bitch,"

"Okay Sakhile, I hear you but what if we do things this way? For starters, I'm not even the one who's -"

Pastor Dube was wheeled onto the broad and massive stage, cast, bandages, the works before being handed a pair of walking sticks by an assistant. Drones circled him and devotees watched in awe as he struggled to stand before addressing his fellow believers of Lucifer's failed attempt in causing any sinister immorality thanks to the protection of his church and the hand of the lord. Finally, disbelievers could see where their money ended up. Not in the belief that it ended up in the pockets of the Pastor, an evil misconception but in protecting one of their own. The lack of animated movements one had come to expect when getting a sermon from Asanda felt out of place, but in the man's defence, they'd covered him in plaster. The service ended with a Dube and not the son of the person they praised and worshipped on everybody's lips. Asking and wondering how he ended up on stage like that. How's being accompanied by who's, why's, when and where to complete the Big 5 of curiousness? Nobody sought answers to these questions more than the siblings that belonged to the Baloyi clan. Looks swapped between each other and an outward look towards his sister revealed a fearful face.

Mandisa's facial expression, despite the common misconception, was not due to mass heaps of paperwork controlling what she could and couldn't do with her body. But knowing that her family's veil of innocence was as fake as the pastor's injuries were real. She found herself caught between two hard surfaces on whether to tell her brother she knew and explain how she found out in the first place or keep quiet, unlike her upcoming child. Mandisa started struggling with fighting off her symptoms. From flu to nausea and everything else that decided to accompany them. Helping Mandisa wasn't anything new nor a problem, but more of a refined task since starting the operation back when she was at school. On this particular occasion, the issue lay with dealing with a culprit who was as easy as picking up a fallen coin with oiled fingers. Mandisa spent her time in and out of the hospital depending on her state of health but also to minimize that of other members of their family from being caught in the crossfire should something unexpected come from the Dube's.

Mandisa made sure to pick the hospitals she'd stay in and for a particular reason. As she sat on her bed, she gripped the hand of the father of her child as they patiently waited for a doctor to arrive. As though she'd been waiting to hear her mind say that, she arrived on cue with a nurse closing the surrounding curtains.

"Evening, my name is Doctor Fezile Zungu, I'll be your obstetrician," she said touching her chest, "And I'll be the one assisting with delivering your baby,"

The pair smiled at each other as their grip on each other tightened as they listened to their doctor regarding the potential complications and an explanation for the unnatural amount of symptoms. With all the information Mandisa would be charged for later, the father of her child spent as much time as could with his would-be family before leaving. The option to disown the child legally was now on the table, but the question was did she?

"Well, well, well, if it isn't the Dube who's supposedly too injured to move?"

The Pastor immediately wondered where the hell his security was in order for him to find himself in such a predicament. The fact that there was no one who could answer meant it was time for some staff to look for some alternative means of employment. Feeling helpless, at something he wasn't even responsible for, all he could do was nod and play along.

"Long time no see, what can I do for you guys, it's been a while," he smiled, waving the cast at them.

"Strip him,"

Without any hesitation, Given did as he was told.

"You've got some nerve going back on stage and performing. I'm surprised you still have the energy,"

"I still got to eat," he sighed.

"You should've mentioned that the first time around, we would've made sure to have left you full. We'll make sure of it this time around, I promise," Emmanuel said, running his hands over the man's eyes before he started beating him through his supposed bandages.

"I only want answers to a few questions, that's all,"

"What!!" the pastor shouted as they continued to bludgeon repeatedly. "Stop," he eventually begged.

"No more bullshit," Emmanuel threatened.

The pastor coughed out blood in agreement before being swarmed with questions, pregnancy included without fail as the picture of how their sister became what she now became clearer.

"Let's start with the sperm, how did you get my sister pregnant?"

"Really, are you seriously going to ask me that?"

Given cracked his knuckles before being held back by his older brother.

"Okay, okay. The sperm injected in her, as one does in normal surrogate procedures and then signs a waiver,"

"And she agreed, just like that. No money, threats, promises, she did it out of the goodness of her heart?"

"Yes, and no... you need to keep in mind that she placed her name amongst a group of several other potential ladies to whom this could've happened to. So it's not like we singled her out. Her name was chosen randomly, lottery style and she became a mother, just like that,"

"And the waiver?"

"What about it?"

"I thought we had an agreement. No more games, I don't have all day to be answering questions. Make it non-existent faster than it appeared," Emmanuel said delicately.

"I don't know," he coughed. "I pray to God I wish I knew, but I don't know. It's not even my sperm we're fighting over," he cried, choking back tears.

"Meaning?"

"I'm infertile," the pastor said after some time.

"Like I said, I don't have time for games. Given, do with him what you will," Emmanuel waved. "tell the big man I said hi,"

The pastor's voice filled the void between the trio as if they were in the middle of praise and worship during one of his sessions before a rude interruption from Emmanuel's voice.

"If you're infertile, how'd you end up with a daughter? I just want to know, for conversation's sake,"

"Because I've always wanted one, just because I can't shoot one out doesn't mean I can't have one. I would've done this procedure if I had the money way back when but she's adopted, by birth but mine by everything else," he cried.

"Fair enough,"

"Then, if it's not your seed, whose is it?"

"As I said, I don't know. You guys will have to do the next logical thing and get a DNA test. But know doing so will put her in jeopardy should things go south because it violates everything she's agreed to,"

"Like we give a shit. Keep talking like the t's and c's of a lottery ticket and that contract and baby won't be the only thing to vanish, as you can see by the members of your beloved security personnel,"

"Get a hold of yourself, you're a grown man. Who's going to have to sort out that mess now?" pointing to the area where the pastor had wet himself.

6

A man with a very swift walk, unperturbed by flashy things around him and the physical embodiment of what not to be tempted by the evils of man. His knocks on Asanda's office were short, sharp and distinct, startling both brothers as we waited in patience to be let in through the open door.

"Doctor Kungwane, here for a... it says here a, Mr A Dube?"

"That's me," said Asanda, spinning on his chair. "How may I be of assistance to you?"

"Is it fine if he's still in the room, or will he give us some privacy?"

"Oh no, not to worry, he's my brother, it's fine you can continue," Asanda smiled.

The doctor opened up his briefcase as he laid it on the table and rummaged around inside for his notes pertaining to his patient before him. He closed the door behind him and began what he'd left the comfort of his own office to come to do. "I'm here to do a follow-up, matter of fact, conclude on an issue that's become of extreme importance. The DNA tests,"

"DNA test?" Sakhile said, speaking out of hand.

"Long story,"

"Don't worry, I got time," Sakhile responded.

"Last time, and you'll correct me if I'm wrong, we ended things off with a cheek swap test and we're now here for stage two, the blood test, correct?"

"That's correct," Dr Kungwane said, in agreement to preparing his workspace.

"Now that you're here, you've got me thinking, why don't you do the both of us? Me, what's missing and my brother over here, both buccal and blood tests in case we have any problems down the line. You saw what the people who you work for are like, so I think it's best to have both our asses covered on this one,"

"I don't think I understand,"

"Nor do I?" Sakhile said from behind, giving his brother an awkward stare.

"Look, man. Look at me... I'm just an injured man trying to make a living preaching the lord's message. Only to lose my life because of some people who don't like what I've been tasked to tell others."

Kungwane gave him an unwelcome stare as his blue gloves echoed across the office as they clapped together against his wrists.

"Look, I'm not going to preach to you, it's after working hours, but what I am going to say to you, no suggest, is that you do both our swabs and something that rhymes with perm," he said, sliding two extremely thick brown paper bags across the table. "This one would ensure that everything that your meticulous and convincing scientific equipment is error-free. And this," pointing at the other packaged between them. "This is to make sure that this conversation never even took place. After all, I am just a struggling pastor trying to get by,"

With that said, the doctor did what he was hired to do and left the Dube's swabbed. If there was one thing Asanda had seen from the man who'd walked into his office with his morals held dear was that he wasn't going to work on Sunday. That statement was a lie; he was going to work. At first, the man was against it, how was he going to whoo his most devoted congregants without miracles, but as he once said while downing a glass of vodka with a surname named 1818 while trying to keep a straight face. But what Asanda soon found out was what he lost out on miracles, he would more than make up for with the pleasures of working from home. That, and the number of new subscribers he had to accustom himself to, no wonder there was a new social media website every time he turned to a new verse. If people could subscribe to Onlyfans, there was nothing stopping him from creating his own and preventing them from subscribing to Holyfans other than a typo from people who were looking for something completely different.

This is not how Mandisa pictured having her baby in the same light nor did Mary picture her son drawing his last breath on a cross. But there she was all alone in the spirit of getting some rest, with the only reminder that she wasn't a virgin when all this happened to her unlike Mary, the fact that she was in a private hospital bed and not a public one all because of him. Her phone rang, yet another call from her mother and she chose to ignore it. Given what had happened the last time she'd chosen to ignore her phone, she completely understood why she already had missed calls sitting in the teens. But she wasn't having it, being shouted at was the last thing she needed, she'd just given birth to a baby for God's sake, something she, herself still had to wrap her head around. Her family had meant well but she knew what she was getting herself into when she signed that non-disclosure, what her family failed to recognise was that it was for her own safety, not just Asanda's peacock tendencies. Why couldn't they just wrap it around their stubborn heads that the more they tried to help her the worse they seemed to make things. Eventually, she found herself being moved from a private room to a public ward, removing her thoughts from the point of insanity and joining five other mothers in different stages of recovery, which was the biggest mistake of her life. This is where she couldn't avoid what needed to be circumvented most, it was during visiting hours when Emmanuel's face made an appearance, making her take note of the actual hours themselves, the smile of the happy emoji wrapped freakishly uncomfortably across his face as he came to see her. He was alone so that was a positive.

One irritating Baloyi was more than enough. Her favourite sweets, flowers and a USB were all sweet gestures, although she didn't understand what the USB was for until he explained it and then she wished she was better off alone than on her surprise visit. To be honest, his childish antics aside, she was happy somebody had come to spend time with her and not go on and on about the baby. If one wanted a surprise for their birthday, there was nothing that beat what she found on the USB. As soon as she started playing it, there was no going back, turning it off of any kind. Their "special gift" aside, Pastor Dube's video played on repeat without any regard for human life other than its own whatsoever. If only he knew how wishing her a speedy recovery would render the opposite of the intended purpose and do nothing but disturb her from watching her favourite show.

Later on that evening

Asanda tried to sit still as he got his bandages redone with the help of his daughter, but the medication used to make his wounds heal did nothing but sting and cause whatever scabs had formed over his wounds to peel off. Although this sent them backwards, all the yapping that came out of it not only served as a moment to bond as a family, but was the perfect small talk they needed before they could address the issue of Asanda's ass-whooping. Faith was right, as much as Asanda hated admitting it, his daughter was right, that footage was all the proof they had that he was still alive. He had taken it for granted, but he didn't realise how traumatic the incident had been for her. A child forced to watch their father nearly killed by two idiots trying to act like gangsters for things that didn't even concern them. Being shot, I'm sure one could get over but run over? What therapist could heal that?

Asanda, realising how close he was to losing the person he loved most in the most traumatic fashion and leaving them with the worst memory of him in their life, gritted through the pain, snarling and clenching his teeth he inched towards his daughter and hugged her. She flinched unexpectedly, not prepared for her father's spur-of-the-moment act of love, but embraced it and melted into his arms with a smile after being kissed on the forehead. What her father did, or rather who her father was when in front of the eyes of his congregation and when with her, were, in essence, Sodom and Gomorrah.

The days that followed

Mandisa's arrival home filled the house and neighbourhood with animosity. Despite having the presence of a newborn baby whose job was to cheer up spirits. Emmanuel somehow found himself serving as the bridge between his sister and the rest of his family, preventing one party from running away and the other from being the reason he did exactly that. If growling was a natural human instinct, Given and Mandisa would do just that when they were placed in close proximity to each other or encountered each other in the lounge as one was passing through. However, one day. One overcast day, a courier stopped by and with it a package no bigger than a bar fridge, but judging by the ease at which the delivery person manoeuvred around it, probably lighter. Stunned, the Baloyi's gathered around it once they were finally alone with it, even Baby Lungelo clutched tightly against the chest of his mother as his head dangled carelessly from her out of interest. Emmanuel tore open to reveal two envelopes that stopped him from going any further. Picking up the smaller of the two letters and tearing it open, he read.

Dear Baloy's

May this find you well, I would sincerely like to apologise for what I have done to your daughter as we do not practise such atrocities in my culture. Please find the following financial contribution towards your home as damages for what I have done to your daughter and if they are not enough, please let me know for me to rectify the insult towards your home immediately.

Signed.

Seeking forgiveness

Emmanuel folded the first and read the second letter attached before handing it over to his sister and addressing the issue of the envelope with damages in it. Mandisa took the letter from her brother gingerly before forcing herself to read what they'd given to her.

Mandisa

First and foremost, I want to thank you for all the courage and strength you've displayed thus far, despite the only thing I've caused in your life is a mess. Also, I do not have the words to thank you enough for allowing me to see our son. I know this isn't much, but I hope this small contribution can help in making Lungelo's life easier.

Ps: Why are nappies so damn expensive?

Signed

Remorseful

As *Remorseful* had hinted, the box was made up of nappies and other things to help ease with raising a baby, a pram, a cot etc. What none of them were anticipating though were damages, they stared at Mandisa waiting for an answer regarding who they were from. But the answer was simple, a non-disclosure prevented her from disclosing who they were from but all she could do was hint that what they were doing was wrong, especially how they went about torturing the pastor since all he was doing was work, similar to how a teacher teaches in a school and doesn't get beaten up for giving a child a bad grade if they do well. Her family would just have to accept it. The silence was heavy but declined as Mandisa attended to her crying child. The Baloyi brothers had had enough of being strung along by this scam of a so-called pastor their mother believed in as much as God and now had managed to wrap their little sister into the same time of belief. If nearly dying wasn't scary enough, then dying would be.

7

The house was eerily quiet when the Baloyi duo moved around the house in the morning like a gecko on the wall, the mist and what little remained of the frost outside accompanying the tone back inside as they prepared to leave. Emmanuel was startled by his mother as they locked eyes in the passage on his way out. She herded her boys towards the lounge to have a seat with her, patting the seat on the couch beside her gently before adjusting her restless grandchild that lay in her other arm before feeding her. Her children relentlessly complied as they found places to sit.

"You know..." she began, "On the one hand, I completely admire and couldn't be prouder as a parent for raising children that know the difference between right and wrong and so motivated by upholding their moral standards. That said, it's contradictory and takes everything I've taught you and throws it in the trash if it's done only when it suits you. Proves more than anything else that being right, unless it's a direction, is subjective and even more so if you're trying to be a superhero. You know what the best part of all of this is?" she asked, looking down at Lungelo and adjusting her bottle. "It's not even your call to make. If Mandisa is actively choosing to be a single parent because that's what the cool kids are doing these days then let that be her mistake to make, not yours to fix," Joyce finished, her eyes moving like the sunrise to its full position from Emmanuel towards Given.

"But Ma," Given began.

"Oh no, let's not get confused, I wasn't asking you, isn't that right?" she asked Faith. "This whoring around she's doing or has done, I don't know, she's a vacuum-sealed container I couldn't tell you even if my life were dependent upon it. Whatever it is she's up to, this much

I know. It too does not sit well with me and take it from me, as a parent, there is nowhere where one has to sign to be obliged to love your child, their decisions, regardless of whether you understand or condone them. What matters is the lesson that comes out of it for the both of you, because if there's one thing that's guaranteed about life is that you'll never stop learning," she said, before preparing to burp her granddaughter.

"But Ma,"

"Yes Ma," Emmanuel finished, speaking over his brother.

"Thank you," she nodded. "It's too cold for this one to be out here and she doesn't want to go to sleep, I don't know why I'm mothering her when she was a mother. Mandisa!" Joyce shouted.

"Ma," she called from the depths of the house before eventually appearing to find her family gathered in the lounge.

"It's too early in the morning for Faith to be this unfaithful to some sleep, please do something about it, I tried what I can remember with you three. It clearly didn't seem to work,"

She did as she was told, ignoring the stares that bore holes into her back, half expecting them to say something to her. She was in and out of that room as quickly as it took most people to skip a YouTube ad and none of them none the wiser why she chose to stick to an NDA and then accept her family's rather uncivilised way of getting out of it.

Meanwhile...

The mist had gone, the frost was no more, and the sun had shown off what it could do before settling down to what it was supposed to do as it began to warm up the earth. A stop at the church revealed the man of the hour unavailable due to injuries and whoever insisted on being a receptionist insisted on leaving a message. Regardless, it was onto Plan B. Since their trip wasn't entirely for nothing as it ended with them in the parking lot disguised as house housing vehicles registered under the Dube-ZN license plate from one to thirteen. Posing as plumbers contracted for one of the many unfinished buildings getting in trouble for being late. First and foremost, and secondly not having their documentation to get them through in order not to make the security personnel job more strenuous than it already was watching out for miscellaneous activities and opening up for delivery men and domestic workers. It took an hour's worth of airtime before the Baloyi's found themselves roaming home.

"This is ridiculous, it's disgusting," clicking his tongue as he shook his head in disappointment, "Look at this," Given continued, pointing around them.

"One day is one day, right," Emmanuel sniggered.

"You got jokes. You forget what your BFF's book says about his lifestyle"

"Ncaw, so what did we learn today?" Emmanuel asked with his hands clasped together and eyebrows wide over his face.

"Proverbs is full of shit but is fully applicable for the sins of this man because he is the personification of greed, blah-blah," he said, before clearing his throat. "As the outstanding book and the magnificently insightful chapter that speaks no wrong says. The ways of people who are greedy find a very swift end,"

"Same chapter also says those who are greedy cause problems in their own home and hate bribes will be okay, so I don't know how this applies to you because you don't fit in either, unless…"

"Say it, I dare you to say it. Say me and that thing are now family and I'll tie both your sperm-deficient dicks together in a knot,"

"Well, that's not a very nice thing to do, or say," Emmanuel sighed as they pulled up on the Dube's driveway, "Especially to family," he laughed before running out of the car.

"Keep talking, you forget between the two of us I'm not the one named after porn," Given pointed.

"Correction. Porn was named after me,"

"Ayi ok, if you say so… who am I to argue with people named last minute, or rather, after last-minute activities that happened after twelve, probably as a testament to their favourite series," Given shrugged.

Emmanuel stormed off and into the Dube's home, leaving his brother bewildered behind him as he tried to catch up. The doorbell and door went from zero to 100 in the time it took startling the inhabitants of the Dube household. The help headed towards the door to find out the source of all the commotion, only to be pushed aside as soon as she opened it to a demand for answers. While Emmanuel shouted his way into the house as he looked for Asanda or Sakhile, Given apologised in his wake. They ignored each other as Emmanuel continued to scream and shout for Asanda as a lost parent in search of their child in a store, only for their child to reveal themselves from nowhere.

After mentally preparing herself for what was to happen after identifying the bullies that tortured her father that fateful day on that car ride. Remembering the day as though it was yesterday. As cliché, as the statement sounded, it was because she could return to the video of the incident whenever emotions got the better of her. Rewatch the moment when she found out she was adopted, not that she had a problem with it but because whoever her actual parents were, couldn't compare to the love that her father had demonstrated in raising her to be who she was today. However, what ate at her the most was being unable to do anything to help her father other than watch. Watch as though he were an ad between her favourite series, unescapable and forced to do so as the soundtrack disappeared and returned.

Yet, here they were, to repeat the gesture. What else were they here to do? It made no sense for them to do anything else. It's not like they were here to be anointed by her father. He'd given them everything that'd wanted, told them everything that they'd demanded and even given them a DNA test against his will to protect his family and yet here they were, in her home. She followed her uninvited guests as they looked for her father, yelling his name throughout the house until they found him, disturbing him from his online sermon as he threw him on the floor. Leaving his chair to spin on its own like a coin deciding whether it was heads or tails.

"Asanda, my mayn," Emmanuel sang as he stared him down before introducing his foot to his chest. "For a disabled man. You sure are a hard man to find, I'll give you that much,"

Asanda stared up at his visitors, their outlines hindered by the light fixture above him on the table he used to keep things illuminated during the sermon. He drew in a deep breath, as hard as it was, only to see his baby girl in the corner of his eye between the legs of his table. A nod assured her he was okay, even though she wasn't convinced it was enough for her to summon the strength to wipe the tears that cascaded down her face, leaving it glowing. His full attention now on his ass-whipping, his prayers for his brother's intervention were finally answered as Sakhile put an end to the bloody mess. And to think all of this could have been avoided if one simple question had been answered. NDA aside, "Who was the father of Mandisa's child?" until they had the answer to that question, his ass-whippings would be given to the only Dube they knew to be the child's other half and then he would go on to give it to whomever he desired to protect so fiercely.

As Dube and Baloyi exchanged directions, the Baloyi's satisfied with a job well done, a pastor encouraged to do the right thing, they left behind three pairs of eyes that stared at them with passion, aggression and endlessly as they moved past each one. Disappearing behind the corner of the door, the Dube's fell into action as Sakhile dropped beside his battered brother who insisted on being okay despite the unhealthy number of times he continued to cough out blood. Even though it was unspoken, Faith was the one responsible for ensuring anybody outside the jagged corners that made up the place she called home knew its true secrets.

She couldn't understand it, no matter how hard she tried to live up to her name or her faith, it all seemed to desert her. Was this so-called miracle baby worth it? Her eyes glazed and glistened as they stared at him in his crumpled state.

"Faith," her uncle repeated, catching her attention the third time around. "I need a minute alone with your father."

She nodded, before slowly making her way out of the room and finding herself tasked with helping with medical assistance. However, her good intentions were disheartened when she found her father and uncle limping down the passage. Although the sight of her father waddling down the corridor was unsettling, it was relieving to hear her family argue. As her father was loaded onto the bed, into an ambulance and off to hospital. She was left alone to figure out whether she had a sibling and if so, the next step from this point onwards. The question was an easy one. The answer, not so much.

8

It was an ordinary day at the hospital only to have it ruined by that thing called Mandisa and the source of all the turmoil in Faith's life. It made no sense why she was here other than the thing she called a child. Chief among these reasons was to make her question whether she had a sibling.

The thought was still incentive enough for her to do something about it, about Mandisa and her necromancy in her life. Motivating her to get rid of that thing that was meant to bring more people to the church, not bring more people full stop. It made no sense why Faith was here if her uncle would ask her to sit outside and rob her of the time allocated to spend with her injured father.

At some point, word got out that they discharged the pastor from the hospital, despite the difficulty in keeping it from the public. Which meant fake smiles all around. Hopefully, food would change things. As they sat in an upmarket restaurant with nothing to spark conversation over other than a child crying. A random attempt by Faith to keep him quiet startled everybody including herself.

The longer she seemed to hold "her brother," the more her feelings towards him changed. His constant visits to the hospital finally made sense, even though Mandisa didn't. She looked into his innocent eyes and wondered what they'd think if they knew what upheaval and emotional distress they'd caused.

"I know right?"

Faith looked at Lungelo, confused at the fact that he could talk with those being his first words.

"Trust me, it's amazing right, what he's able to do?" Mandisa asked.

"Excuse me?"

"I can tell by the way you're looking at him, that you understand what it's like to go through a lot and still smile like there's nothing wrong,"

Faith nodded softly.

"That one right there is quite a handful," Mandisa sighed.

"And I've been dealing with my dad," Faith said softly, choosing her words carefully.

"When he puts the bottle down, he's amazing,"

Faith rolled her eyes at her.

"If you ever want to trade, don't hesitate to call me," Mandisa said, waving her hand urgently before accepting Lungelo back.

However

What was intended as a trade turned into a visit. One private visit after another, without the knowledge of Mandisa's brother's and Faith's father. The two spending forbidden time with one another united by none other than Lungelo. The opportunity to kill Mandisa had never been easier than now. To silence her forever and get rid of all the problems she'd brought along with her, but... the commitment to do so was a complicated one.

Impossible....

It was a cold Saturday morning, with Faith cradling Lungelo on her back, practising to be a mother even though she didn't want children even when the time came. But in her defence, it was the best way to shut up Lungelo while his mother was busy. Dr Zungu this, Dr Zungu that, for someone who just wanted to go to the doctor and get it over and done with. Even when they eventually made it to the miracle obstetrician, whatever that was.

"And who might we have here?" she asked, adjusting her glasses.

"My niece," Mandisa said, once she and Faith had exchanged looks.

"How very nice of her to join us," Dr Zungu smiled, "And the father of the child?"

"Business,"

"Very well. As you know, our journey together was for the delivery of your baby. Now that's been a success, it seems that our post-natal care journey has come to an end. But to ensure the likelihood that we avoid any complications, mainly high blood pressure since Lungelo wasn't a vaginal delivery, but a caesarean. Oh, and a miscarriage, you can come back for a foetal assessment but you are well within your rights to see another physician for a second opinion,"

"You mentioned something about depression?"

"In all probability, due to the inability to have a natural childbirth and as we've discussed, it's completely normal. It wouldn't be if it were the latter, but it seems that you're healthy. But keep in mind your mental health determines the health of your baby boy."

And to think all she did was just smile in front of a pastor and expect a miracle as if that's how they worked. Instead of harassing her family in search of unredeemable good. She was meant to focus on her own family, harness all that energy she had left towards the father of her child and work together to create a brighter future for Lungelo.

"And my uncle?"

"What about him?" Dr Zungu asked in confusion.

"Does he know about this, will you tell him this complicated version or is it my aunt's job?" Faith asked, pointing at Mandisa.

"You raise a good point, little girl. Mandy would you like me to tell,"

"No, it's fine," she said, startling Lungelo. "I'll just give him the simplified version, I know how he hates listening to explanations," she finished as she soothed her child.

"Very well," the doctor nodded.

Faith stared precariously at the child in front of her as the rest of the appointment continued and headed home once it was done. She was a much wiser woman then than when she'd begun her day, however, the question still remained whether to speak or wait for what had essentially become her aunt to speak first.

9

"Renowned and controversial church leader of the Dube Church of True Believers in Durban has been left in a critical condition in hospital after a failed assassination attempt in his private residence. The matter is still under investigation according to a police spokesperson. What Detective Anita Xaba has told the SABC is that the estate's security guards are one of the leading suspects in this case. Furthermore, the lack of any sign of Pastor Dube should be no reason for alarm until an official statement has been issued by the police or his family and thus both parties would urge devoted worshipers that there is no need for violence and riots. For further developments and updates on this story follow us on our website and social media platforms. This has been Luyanda Mthethwa saying goodnight,"

"You hear that, they called me renowned," Asanda gleamed.

"They also called you controversial," Sakhile replied.

"You're just jealous because you weren't mentioned," he said, sticking out his hand. "Entertaining kids aside, do you have any good news for me, doctor?"

"I'm afraid not, but the DNA tests were successful and I've tracked down the child's father, matter of fact, I have him here with us,"

"Perfect," Asanda gasped, rubbing his hands together.

"Would you like to meet him?" Kungwane asked, pointing at the door.

"Do kids colour water blue when depicting it?"

"A simple yes would've sufficed, Asanda?" Sakhile sighed.

"Wena, stop asking me useless things and answer questions of importance, do you have an NDA?"

"Is there any other way?"

"They should've just named you the NDA brothers," Kungwane mumbled as he fetched their guest. "Dube my ass,"

When he returned, Sakhile turned down the tv as it continued to mumble on about how his brother ended up in the hospital. What he saw was the last thing he had in mind. But then again, it wasn't his DNA, so it served him right for the assumption. What was going to be undertaken was going to be a huge step for everybody involved. Dr Kungwane's pay check would come to an end, Lungelo's father's sins would finally catch up to him and all of this would happen at the expense of the Dube's, a punching bag for the Baloyi's due to their sibling's trollop ways.

With that said, Asanda might've been in hospital, fighting for a proper grip on his life, but it didn't mean that miracles had to stop happening in any way, shape or form.

A few weeks later...

Police surrounded the main road leading onto the freeway and intersections surrounding DCTB. Ushering cars around and helping them find alternative routes to the church despite their final destinations being hindered by the church itself. Meanwhile, Sakhile and whatever legal assistance he could assemble on short notice on a Sunday were doing their level best in trying to mitigate a fine for public disturbance or at the very least, try their level best not to get arrested. Just like the City of Durban and the police, they had not prepared for their church to overflow with this many people, all of them knew Asanda had some level of fame but prior to his hospitalisation and post, it was as good as knowing who Jesus was before and after he'd been crucified. With jail avoided, all Sakhile had to ensure was that they didn't end up in one himself because whether Asanda wanted to admit it or not, performing acts of God in orange overalls was extremely difficult.

Finding the words to describe what it was like to roll alongside an individual as anointed as Asanda were, but the roar of his believers as they saw him limp onto the middle of the stage was one of them. Feeling solid concrete vibrate as they chanted his name, giving him the idea of what it felt like to be lightning in a cloud of thunder before being expelled was another. After all, what sounded like screaming to one brother were merely hymns to another. Asanda raised his hand, calming his excited crowd swiftly before introducing them to a well-rehearsed speech about his eager return and, as a result, his true reason for being there.

"True believers, I'm here to share wisdom and knowledge. Those who know of Dube know he is a messenger and is forbidden to hide the truth. I've been rewarded. I've been shown things and been to the other side where I'd be unable to fake them even if I'd been given all the resources in the world to try. Despite all the technology we have,"

"Amen!" the crowd boomed.

"Just as they foretold in Deuteronomy 18:18 when it describes of a prophet whom God would speak through. A prophet who's expected to perform miracles like Moses and to lead people to follow God. I am that prophet. That placeholder the Lord has placed before the return of Jesus," Pastor Dube cried.

"Amen,"

"Because of this unspoken anointing, I've been blessed with the unspeakable. The impossible. The ability to perform a miracle only foretold in the old testament. I have been blessed with the permission to raise a man from the dead,"

The church went quiet and Dube waited patiently for the murmurs of disbelief to stop from those who thought he was talking complete bullshit, perfectly hidden, allowing them to doubt their leader in confidence. Once the building was quiet, he could continue.

"When I say I've been to the other side, do not get me wrong. I am not the lord. I am in no position to be placed on a cross so put down your tools, I have merely been granted the ability by the almighty

Father to see and do things like he during his three days away from earth. After his sacrifice for you and I,"

"Amen,"

"But you and I know I am a man of brief words," pointing at his chest. "And therefore, let my actions do the talking, which is why we are all gathered here today. Please, will you all welcome Dr Lebo Kungwane," he said, with an outstretched hand that swivelled behind him, revealing a man with a coffin behind him. To some, it looked as if he tried to out-walk the box raising no attention to himself. "Could you please tell us your reason for being here?"

"My name is Dr Lebo Kungwane, I am a..." thinking of a title, "forensic pathologist," he finished.

"Wow sounds interesting, and could you please tell us a little about what your job is about, you know, inspire the youth in our Sunday School to aspire to be more than just doctors,"

"Pathology is a broad subject, for example, not everybody who studies theology is called a pastor but the subject itself is the study of disease. As a forensic pathologist, my focus is on studying how people died and..."

"Yeah, sure whatever sounds interesting. Now, tell me, what is the cause of death of this man?" Dube asked, prying open the coffin. "And can you confirm he is dead and how?"

"High blood pressure, If you would like to turn your toys away for this part as it might be too gruesome for sensitive viewers. As you can see here, the subject has fixed eyes and has not blinked for an extended period rendering them cloudy and dry. Relaxed muscles have rendered the skin loose and we can say the greenish tinge here around his fingers is a sign of decomposition. Something I should look into actually," the doctor finished, placing the deceased finger back down.

"Now, followers of God's practice, there you have it, first-hand from a man of science, a heathen that is yet to accept the message of God. Now kind sir, if you will, please assist me in resurrecting this man from the dead as I can't seem to locate a nurse to assist me in doing this anywhere," Dube sighed.

"Excuse me?"

"Don't be afraid, your role is insignificant like the carpenter who created the cross for our lord and Saviour,"

"Amen," the church sang.

"Uh... what am I supposed to do?" Lebo asked, scratching the back of his head.

"Just hold this man here," pointing at his shoulders, "and after a short prayer, I've been given to recite, twist and pull as hard as you can until you hear a clicking sound. Make sense?"

Lebo nodded.

"We will then do this for his four major limbs and let his faith and the power of God take over from there," Asanda finished, pointing at his knees and remaining shoulder.

And so Doctor and Priest's arms took their place on the corpse in preparation to perform a revival, to do things that were only renowned in the fiction and not truth. Soon silence followed, the church went dim, and a spotlight hovered on the stage above Lebo and Asanda as they began to operate.

Grab and twist.

There was a scream from inside the box as they acted.

"You idiot," Asanda whispered. "You were only supposed to pretend to twist," before shouting Amen "It's Okay, no reason to be alarmed. No reason to scream doctor, you might worry our most devoted of followers," Asanda smiled. "Now let's try again,"

His devotees gave motivational applause before Doctor Lebo took hold of another arm to perform yet another miracle. Silence, a prayer and a click soon followed before the remaining limbs were finished and the doctor applauded for his participation. What was left now was for Asanda to finish what he'd started. He now had the pieces of the puzzle assembled and all that remained was to show everybody else what the image looked like once arranged. He wiped his brow and his followers watched as anxiously as he was. Taking a deep breath was all that was left for him to recite a small prayer over the man that lay in the coffin. His eyes fixed, unwavering, like the film projected by the drone above, a prayer which was the code name agreed upon for the man to stand up and as promised the man rose from his tomb and stood on his own two feet, stunning both church and pastor.

Dube's Church of True Believers lost their mind, faith and in some cases, voices when they couldn't believe that they'd been part of a miracle. Something people wouldn't believe when they were told, be it by word of mouth or had paid for the evidential footage thanks to the taping by the ingenuity of their pastor. Claiming it was fake or photoshopped, it didn't matter, things that were often true and revolutionary were often placed under the same blanket.

"So who are you, from where you've come other than a tomb in my church?" Asanda cried.

"You know of me, albeit I tend to keep to myself around you,"

"Excuse me? I don't think I understand,"

"I know of you more than you think I do or supposed to," he said. Lebo has a loose mouth when he'd drank.

"You're not making sense," scratching the back of his head before turning to face his church. "I guess raising people from the dead isn't an exact science and shouldn't be tried at home," he joked.

"How many people here know about Faith?"

Asanda swivelled around as though he had no neck with his security team not even waiting for a signal before jumping onto the floor again, taking care of him despite him putting up a fight.

"At least let me tell you who I am, let me not be a waste of your money. I hunted Lebo down specifically for this job," he said between the arms of two men that dragged him away and stopped waiting to confirm from their employer whether they should give this... whatever they were yet to call him but crazy wasn't it, a chance to speak. He nodded, and they stopped abruptly as a taxi would when finding a passenger on the side of the road.

"My name is Spha. Sphamandla Dlamini and I'm the father of Mandisa Baloyi's child

10

J oyce who had decided to watch the ceremony online rather than attend it was flabbergasted. She was out of words, even when she turned around to face her daughter, it wasn't out of judgement but out of pure shock. More than anything she was confused and hurt on why her daughter wouldn't share something so life-changing and massive in their lives with her but as she looked around. Her spirit slowly found its way back towards her body, realising that she wasn't the only one who felt the way she did as Mandisa and her siblings stood there, open-mouthed as though they were sculpted water fountains with no water to give.

"And then?" she said, filling the house with shock.

"Haibo! I'm as confused as you are. I don't know who this person is. It's the first time I've seen them in my life and besides, even if it were true, it wouldn't happen because he's not my type. A forehead like that would give me ugly babies for starters,"

"Denial is the first step to admitting you have a problem sis," Emmanuel said softly, rubbing his hand across her shoulder.

"Hey, fuck off!"

"That's it, let it out,"

"Remember, we're family, we're here to support you, that's what families do," Given smiled, arms wide open, ready to embrace his sister in a hug.

"Stop,"

"Shh, let us help, we've helped you get Lungelo's father off your shoulders, who's sorry, what's next?" Given asked.

"I'm warning you, stop," she said, pointing at each of them.

"Anger is not the way," Emmanuel smiled, stifling a laugh.

"Okay, enough you two, leave your sister alone. Mandisa you also need to stop parading this child of yours like all your naked peers on Insta what-what you're always on. How are you supposed to be a decent mother when your attention is fixed on your phone trying to look for a father for your child than on your child itself,"

Mandisa fell silent. She realised that she was better off agreeing to whomever the person online claiming to be Lungelo's father was from the get-go than trying to win this argument. Why did she think experience would decide to change direction all of a sudden? However, on the bright side, her son now had a father that her family and everybody else would stop pestering her about. Meanwhile, back in the lounge, the mood had changed as the Baloyi's came to terms with what they'd almost done, provided what they'd just watched was actually true. For starters, they almost took got rid of their mother's favourite non-definitive person and beside's asking the Big D for living up to his side of the promise there was a lot to find out about this new Sphamandla character in order to make him disappear as fast as he appeared.

Meanwhile

"What the fuck was that?" Asanda screamed, slapping his fists on the table.

"What was what?" the doctor asked.

"Don't you get smart with me, just because we re-enacted a rise from the dead doesn't mean I can't put a real one in there," pointing across the table at his guest.

"Listen, I'm just as surprised as you are, I don't get to choose them but all I can say is, you get what you pay for," Kungwane said, shrugging. "Next time, slide a bigger envelope that's all I can say before I love and leave you. Thank you very much for your hospitality, but this time around I think I'll see myself out,"

"I've had it. I've had it up to here with that piece of shit," Asanda said with an unrecognisable voice.

"Want me to find us a new doctor?" Sakhile asked.

"No, it'll take forever to get them to keep their mouth shut enough to allow us to preach to the masses with confidence. Besides, we need everybody now more than ever, that reminds me. Who's this fella who knows about our NDA's or has she broken it because if she has then... oh well, she seemed truthful, but then again you think you know a person, right?" turning towards Sakhile.

"Right," his brother nodded, putting his phone down.

Faith waited for her father to finish up in the office with his work. An old man popped out unanticipated, it wasn't long before her uncle did the same and then she knew that it was time to go home as her father would be next any minute now. The ridged brown door reminded her of the events that had happened earlier today when a man claimed to be Mandisa's father when clearly wasn't. She knew exactly who he was, I mean Hello!! They went to the doctor with him on several occasions. The question was, did Mandisa know about this or better still, was this something done by the couple to further themselves from one another? The more she thought about it the more she confused herself, finding herself entering a matrix of questions until she decided the best thing to do, the only thing to do was ignore herself like the message on her phone that lay lonely, cold and ignored, a complete no-no for any message.

When news broke of how they had terrorised, intimidated and threatened the poor Dube family, most particularly Asanda Dube and as a result, he was unable to perform his job properly and most likely the reason the news of the father of one of his congregants slipped his mind because it was simply devoted elsewhere. When accused of shifting the blame elsewhere, video footage shot by faith proved otherwise, but it came at a cost. The first was that the entire world knew that the miracle involving Mandisa Baloyi was faked meaning it put all of his other miracles into question and gave the Baloyi family a leg to stand on. Even though it didn't justify their actions and legitimize them, they made sense, meaning that they didn't come out of the blue. This resulted in a #TeamBaloyi on social media from all those who were all for it, seeing their version of events as David slaying Goliath that was Dube. The Baloyi's stuck around long enough to find out that they were responsible for Pastor Dube's medical bills. Which made no sense for a man who claimed he was fully healed thanks to the love and prayers, and more importantly, the financial help from all of his unwavering devotees.

Unexpected news when all it did was leave your family in shock and even more unexpected when it rendered brutal knocks on the door followed by the words, "Police, open up!"

An awkward silence emerged around the house as each family member looked at one another, almost as though passing the blame from one person to the next for the arrival of the law. What's more, just when they needed each other most, to bind together in an effort of unwavering silence, Lungelo broke all that nonsense as he cried for his mother's attention in need of a bottle of milk, not only helping himself with much-needed nourishment but revealing her from the confusion she found herself in that she had nothing to do with. The police's knocks on the door were brutal but not as brutal as how Emmanuel yanked it over, leaving one of them to stumble inside, tripping over himself before he'd finished knocking.

"Can I help you?"

"Futsek wena," the cop said, pushing him aside and letting himself in before making way for his colleague to follow from behind.

Irritated and not in the mood for games, it was a quick flash of his badge, and just as quick to place the Baloyi brothers in the back of the police vehicle. Leaving mother and daughter confused as they were scared, despite having everything explained to them on multiple occasions. Getting arrested was nothing like it was on tv, even more so in South Africa, no, "I'll call my lawyer," no rules about what they could and couldn't do to you and even if they were the law they were treated more than just suggestions. After all, being chucked around in a newly spray-painted bakkie, slightly modified for ventilation for whatever it was shuffling around wasn't exactly class-leading for moving about offenders, falsely accused or otherwise. It felt as though the route with the most speedbumps and potholes was chosen to make those at the back rattle, shake and jump as though they were freshly popped popcorn rendering them two different sets of people from the point they'd entered the van to the point they'd been forced out.

Meanwhile, back at the house, as the women gathered their barring's they realised that there was nothing they could do about it now, they didn't even have a family lawyer nor have the funds to acquire one on standby. Joyce's beloved boys would have to wait until the beginning of the week before she could do anything that involved assistance so until then, her boys would have to get acquainted with jail and learn to differentiate the difference between it and prison. While her mother came to terms with what happened to her children, Mandisa refused to accept it. She was on the phone as much as her mother was off it, pulling strings whichever way she could and in that time boy did she learn how to sow. Sowing enough to find out and then cover up the whereabouts of Faith since all she left was a riddled text message and no response. Much needed time with the love of her life and speaking of love, a chance to sit down with the man who claimed to be the love of her life back to be reunited with her. A scary thought but a romantic gesture in any novel and telenovela.

11

I t was a calm Saturday like any other when Lungelo had a family outing with his parents. To those looking from the outside, they were the object of envy, unaware of all the things hidden under the carpet to keep up appearances.

Nevertheless, now was not the time to think of what could've been but just enjoy the moment for what it was and even though he was an infant. All he could do at this stage was listen to his parents' conversations and come to find out that as he grew, he'd get to hear less and less of them.

"So listen, I'm not sure if you've heard the news lately," Mandisa began, clearing her throat.

"Ha, even the deaf couldn't miss out on the action you've managed to provide,"

She rolled her eyes before looking at him hesitantly in the eye. "I need help,"

"Now that's a first,"

"You know what, never mind," she sighed, gathering her things.

"Ag no man, you know I'm only playing. It's been so long, I haven't seen you since the sun figured out it was hot," he smiled, rubbing his hand across her cheek as he turned it towards him.

"I need help, I've never done this before and it's my first time so it's okay if you say no, I completely understand. I've given this a whole lot of thought before bringing it up,"

"What is it, babe?"

She looked at him, her eyes wavering as the only physical piece of evidence of her mental battle of whether to tell him or not. "I need money," she whispered.

"What?"

"I need money," sounding much more audible the second time around.

"Oh, don't worry, I heard you clearly the first time. I just didn't peg you to be that type of woman," scratching the back of his head as a reflex to the state of shock he was in.

"And what type is that?"

"Uh...you know?" he shrugged.

"No, I don't. If I didn't, I wouldn't have asked now would I?" Mandisa growled, ignoring her partner's cries of discomfort.

"What the fuck for, I mean how much?"

"I think I've got my answer, but thanks for your help,"

"Huh?"

"Also, it's getting late, I think it's time Lungelo and I get going, it was fun hanging out, hopefully, we can do this again sometime," she said, packing up her things and stuffing them in the bag with all the baby's necessities.

"What do you mean sometime again? He's my son not an attraction at a theme park and the sun hasn't even fucking gone down yet. What shit are you smoking about it being late?" he asked amongst question after question as he watched her get ready to leave him like he'd been stood up.

She ignored him like a person accustomed to the radio on only to have some noise in the house. She gave her surroundings one last look before wrapping Lungelo around her back and standing up to leave.

"Mandisa, I'm talking to you," he said, grabbing her arm.

She let out a loud scream. It attracted eyes and attention to her, startled her child and started him off on a path of no return as he began to cry. But most importantly, forced her kidnapper to let go of her before turning all of her attention on convincing Lungelo.

On the trip home, she remembered other commitments she'd made a plan to. She quickly called her friend to see whether they were still on and too late to cancel, her mind still distracted by what had recently happened to make up an excuse, taking Lungelo home now would render her too late to pitch up in the first place so they'd just have to suck it up if they were uncomfortable with him being there. Besides, she'd be extra cautious, he was after all her baby and she'd make sure nothing would happen to him. She'd arrived in Yellowwood Park and as per usual whenever she chose to remain in the car while she claimed to be coming from her block of flats, surprise, surprise. She didn't. As she waited, Mandisa wondered why the suburb was so revered. Sure, they built it far from factories, unlike Montclair down the hill. But it didn't justify the property values of the area when most of the scenery was freeways and bush.

"Ya Sfebe, what you waiting for, let's go," Nodumo said, slamming the car door behind her.

"Shh! You'll wake up Lungelo," pointing behind her.

"Sorry," she whispered amongst apologetic body gestures. "Anyway, do you really want to do this?"

"Is there any other option?"

"Oh, I don't know- not doing it in the first place seems to be the first one that comes to mind," Nodumo shrugged /shaking her head in disappointment. "You want another because I could keep going like a scratched cd?"

"Why are we meeting this person in the first place, and more importantly, where are we meeting him?"

"I don't know, one of those fancy restaurants in Gateway, but pass me my phone with the blue cover so I can confirm,"

"Ey you and so many phones, God knows why when you can just carry one that takes dual sim cards. You look like a loan shark, what's the code for this heavy hunk of junk of yours?"

"2022"

"Ncaw"

"Fuck off,"

"Okay, it says here, we're going to Gateway, News Cafe or Primi. Please confirm,"

Nodumo repeated, reading the message out loud.

"Oh crap, I forgot," Mandisa cried, slamming her hand on the steering wheel.

"Oh well, there's always the option to go to KFC if the two can't decide on where to go,"

Nodumo smiled, amused at her own joke. "Anyway, I'm just going to say keep it simple

and don't try to keep up appearances and out of your league, it's not worth it and appearance,"

"Speaking from experience?"

"Yep, and Lungelo?"

"Hey, that's your problem, not mine, you're the one who decided to bring him along,"

Nodumo shrugged, waving her hands around and absolving herself of taking up any responsibility. Before Mandisa had a chance to answer her phone rang, for what must've been the umpteenth time that day and she immediately switched it off, having heard enough of it ring.

"And then?"

"Let's focus on one thing at a time,"

"Yes my queen," Nodumo bowed.

Soon the trio was at the mall but due to the time of day and not all of them being of age, venues changed but not to KFC. Mandisa had already made up her mind, it was either now or never, after all, she'd already been through, Nodumo getting cold feet on her own suggestion and one disappointment after the other, the only positive thing that seemed to happen was finding a seat at the food court.

Their guest walked up to them respectfully, leaving Nodumo speechless as his voice caused her to blush. "The name is Spha," he greeted with one arm outstretched and the other on his chest.

"We know," Nodumo replied before pushing the outstretched hand in front of her toward

Mandisa and ignoring her side-eye.

"Mandisa," she nodded, shaking it. "Please ignore her, she hasn't had sex in a while,"

"And who's this cute fella?" she asked.

"Don't worry yourself about him, let's get down to business and focus on why we're here," Mandisa replied, pulling Lungelo away from him and handing him over to Nodumo before the three of them found a seat.

"So, where would you like for me to start?" Spha asked.

"The beginning sounds like a great place to start," Nodumo scoffed.

12

Finding an audible place to sit amongst the noise wasn't an easy task but once they'd found one it was swiftly down to business. Sphamandla Dlamini, who was he? Why was he here? And most importantly, what did he want with Mandisa Baloyi? Questions that seemed easy to ask and get answers to while Nodumo and her friend formulated them in the car but proved to be a much more unfamiliar task once their prime suspect was within arm's reach. How it came to be that she was sitting here, alive, was a glitch in the matrix and the more Mandisa thought about Spha's tale, the harder she found it to believe. Not due to it being fabricated or complete bullshit, but just at the sheer irony and wonder. But above all else, how she was still alive as he continued to explain his situation.

A few moments ago

So not to put any words in Spha's mouth, but this is how he came to be Ms Baloyi's husband or to put it legally, how Ms Baloyi came to be Mrs Dlamini. It all started at the sermon at the DCTB when Minister Dube professed he could make someone pregnant out of the blue. He'd been drinking with a couple of friends the night before and couldn't go home so he decided to sleep the night off at his house. Unannounced to him, he found out the following morning that his friend was a staunch believer in Dube, whom he thought was complete bullshit. They got into an argument about whether Mandisa would fall pregnant and how she'd fall pregnant if she were somehow miraculously were to. Having watched the sermon online, they put their money where their mouths were and bet on her through 'donations', R450 over R400, allegedly, the highest for the sermon for the day, with no prizes on who donated the extra R50, a hand on his chest. That was meant to be the end of that, however...

Mandisa took offence to the story but continued to listen in silence while Nodumo took over the job of being her mouth while she lost the ability to speak. But with her inability to speak, she didn't allow it to prevent her from hearing the rest of the story as it was about none other than her. So she listened intently as Spha continued, telling Nodumo and her how he carried on with normal life until a couple of months later, he was contacted by a doctor who needed to meet with him regarding an urgent situation regarding his health. Getting what he deserved for ignoring his instincts, he arrived at what looked like a general practitioner's office.

"Name?" Nodumo interrupted.

"Ntombela, a Ntando Ntombela, if I recall correctly. She checked and gave me a free consultation. It all seemed pretty standard except for the lack of payment. After a few visits, she introduced me to a new doctor -"

"Name?"

"Uh...Kungwane, I if I'm right,"

"We need facts pretty boy, not hearsay,"

"It was a Kungwane because I remember when we met he emphasised how much I shouldn't worry and how he'd correct me to what he was whenever I called him a doctor,"

"And what was that?"

"A geneticist,"

"Go on," Nodumo waved.

"So I went to see the geneticist who took my DNA after signing an unbroken string of paperwork, again... I'm just summarising here. At some point, he took a sample of my sperm before realising the biggest bombshell of my life, that I was a father. Initially, I didn't trust him, nobody would've in their right state of mind but the genetic proof was there, I was a dad. At first, it didn't bother me being a sperm donor and all but the longer the thought stayed the more it ate at me and soon I was torn between doing the right thing for my child even though I hadn't seen it, known its existence until a few months ago and just letting it all go because I was thinking too much into this. Obviously, I asked the doctor to help, he said no, showed me the paperwork where I'd signed why I shouldn't and couldn't look for my unborn child."

Mandisa played with Lungelo, rocking him back and forth in her arms as she listened. Her eyes fixed on the man that sat opposite her. It made it extremely difficult for him not to feel awkward or establish any eye contact.

"So, how do we find ourselves here?"

"Same doctor, different consultation, your beloved pastor interrupted it. Well, they didn't exactly barge in but they stole the time I was meant to go in, delaying my day since I had to wait for them to finish. Anyway, I went in the doctor seemed shaken up, I saw an envelope which I assume was money indicating some shady shit had gone down. I kept my mouth shut and minded my own business because that's how the good guys live in the movies."

He offered to keep my secret, so I asked for the identity of my child. I sold my car and used the money to buy a smaller one. I split the rest between paying the doctor and saving for my child.

Mandisa clutched her child tightly towards her chest.

"So I was promised to get paid by the pastor if I did something for him and-"

"Why him and how much?" Mandisa asked.

"Three times what I'd paid to the geneticist to get the details of my child and before you ask, I'd forked out R50 000 to know the identity of my child, its whereabouts, mother and what was currently going on in its life to establish whether it was taken care of before making any moves of my own. It seemed like a fool proof request at the time, vele-vele the man was infertile, I had the documentation and the sperm to prove that the child was mine," pointing at Lungelo, "And most importantly, I'd get paid R150 000 for it,"

"What makes you think this child is yours? I've had a long day, please don't start any shit with me. I'm not one of your idiotic doctors," Nodumo pointed.

"I'm not an idiot,"

They looked at him awkwardly.

"First and foremost, nobody brings a child to a negotiation and secondly, nobody keeps clutching it every time it's mentioned,"

"So what do you want?" Nodumo demanded.

"Nothing, just rights to see my child, that's all. As any logical parent would," Spha said calmly. Well, as calmly as the surrounding scenery would allow.

"Fair enough,"

"Oh, and there is one more thing," pivoting backwards as he got ready to leave.

They watched him as he spun around, bracing for what he'd say next.

"I'm going to need full custody of our child, thanks," giving a courteous nod.

"Sorry?" Mandisa asked.

"I would repeat myself but I think it's safe to say you heard me the first time. I'm just not sure whether you want to discuss a date of exchange now or-"

"Forget it Mafiki'zolo, it's not happening," she said with an index finger separating the two of them.

"Sisi, please. Don't make this harder than it already is,"

"There is no way in hell I'm letting you take my child,"

"Then I guess you need to book a ticket since they're currently on special while we're still in winter,"

"And you'd know all about that, wouldn't you, Satan?"

"Listen, you seem like a nice person but if you honestly think you're going to win this fight over me when I managed to render a person known to the entire country as tasteless as an egg sandwich forced to go cold in a child's lunchbox then you've got another thing coming,"

"Oh trust me, it's not the battle you should be worried about...but the war,"

"Goodbye," Nodumo waved.

"What's that supposed to mean?" Spha asked.

"It means goodbye," Nodumo waved.

"Till we meet again ladies. Hopefully, under better circumstances," Spha waved as he left.

"Goodbye," Nodumo clicked her tongue as they watched Satan disappear. "So... Lungelo and him sharing the same DNA, could you imagine? You going to make it happen?"

"Nope,"

"You're not even going to think about it?" she asked as they headed towards the car.

"You want to walk home?"

"No,"

"You don't even want to think about it?" Mandisa asked

"Okay, I see your point,"

It would be a straightforward drive back to Yellowwood Park to return Nodumo back to her place before heading back home herself and catch some much-needed rest from all the commotion that had ensued. She'd start afresh the next day, hopefully forgetting the events that happened the previous day. But nothing was ever straightforward when Nodumo was involved. Snooping around, she came across one of Mandisa's phones and got to work, quiet about her deception in the exact same manner as she was told to keep quiet while her friend answered the phone. Tipsy and filled with nicotine.

"Mandisa,"

"Ma?" she replied before pointing a stern finger at Nodumo.

"Where are you? I've been trying to call you the whole day,"

"Sorry, my battery went flat, I've managed to get it charged. What's wrong are you, okay, you sound uneasy,"

"No, I wanted to tell you the good news, your brothers are out of jail,"

"How!"

"I don't know, I'm just grateful to God that my prayers were answered. My boys are going to sleep at home tonight and that's all that matters right now,"

"I don't understand. What do you mean Given and Emmanuel are out of jail, how? Who paid bail for them? I'm so confused, in fact, where are you now?" Mandisa asked.

"You ask so many questions my baby. You know you should've been a lawyer. I'm in jail with them as we speak, I'm just waiting for them to get their things since this all happened so suddenly, you know,"

"So, how are you getting home? Is Given or Emmanuel going to pay for an Uber for you guys to head home or use your phone, what's happening?"

"Praise Jesus, you answered because I don't know, I took the phone you and your brothers call the brick because I didn't want anything to happen to mine. So please come fetch us?" Joyce asked nervously.

"Where are you?"

"Westville prison. Please hurry, this place makes me feel uncomfortable,"

"Okay, coming Ma," and hung up before turning towards her friend who realised the amount of space in the car. She ignored her friend's stares as she changed direction on the highway and drove towards prison.

"I guess this means we shouldn't take the freeway on our way back to avoid police," Nodumo suggested, looking at the road in front of her and breaking the ice that was in the car.

"To my beloved gps, how helpful of you," Mandisa answered.

13

The car ride home might have been awkward and a bit over-cramped but if you wanted free peace of mind, nothing beat home and boy did Given miss it. Demanding answers from his younger sister that she herself hadn't the slightest clue of. Who had posted bail was the question on every single individual's lips, Baloyi's or not. With enough persuasion, Nodumo agreed to take a cab home, leaving Mandisa's laundry to air out with confidence and without fear. Being accused of being a whore was nothing new. She often had the facts to disprove her accuser's accusations. That said, it didn't mean because she couldn't provide any information regarding her family's bail that she'd sleep around to find out. Not even 24 hours had passed since they'd physically met and yet, he was able to torment her as she kept looking at her phone, expecting him to call the same way a teenage girl would, anxious of being stood up. Her mind halfway back from the psychiatric hospital, she plucked up the courage to do something no other woman in their right mind would do. But that's the problem, she wasn't in her right mind as she listened to the phone ring. She'd done something she'd sworn she'd never do and when the man on the other end answered, he sounded calm, if not automated enough to give directions.

"Hello, to you too," he began.

"Ag, not this shit. What is it, what haven't I done, I've done everything you've asked me to do. Why can't you do the one thing I've asked and just leave me alone?"

"Your family okay, you guys make it back home safely,"

"Leave them out of this, I've left out yours. I think mine deserves the same kind of respect," she said, clicking her tongue.

"Fair enough, but I still need to see you, we have some unresolved business we need to take care of, especially if this is how you now feel about me. Especially since it's out of the blue which I don't understand. That, I'm afraid, you'll have to make me understand,"

"Fine,"

"Great. Just tell Lu-" Mandisa dropped the phone and sighed loudly as she ran her hands down her head. How did she get herself in this mess, how the hell would she be able to explain that her son had two fathers even though she'd slept with none of them? When that uneventful day did decide to arrive and he wanted to know what his paternal lineage looked like even though in all honesty it didn't exist. What son in their right mind would believe that they didn't have a father when everybody else around him ran around with one or at the very least someone from their father's side of the family? The only answer she had was that he, Lungelo Baloyi, was a miracle baby and that was the truth, no matter how much it sounded like a lie.

The days that followed included a mood or for a lack of a better word a vibe that was tense in the Baloyi household. Despite Joyce's best efforts to resolve it among her children, she decided that they were old enough to resolve their own problems as long as they kept them out of it and out of her house. Given had decided that they needed to pay God's heaven on earth a visit but was on the fence on whether he should do it alone or with Emmanuel given the results of the last time they went to 'talk' with the poor man. The man was healthy, if anything, all he needed now was to record a video of himself dancing and post it online to show the world how much he'd returned to his former health and state of now a qualified extortionist.

If there's anything he could take back, it's the way he went about it with his daughter as she had nothing to do with this but hey... lesson learned. He sat quietly in the lounge and allowed the sound of the tv to fill the house while he thought. Drowned deep in his thoughts he didn't notice his sister leave, walking right passed him as she headed for the front door and out of the house. Gone. Poof. No more, only to resurface at the doctor's room of Doctor Zungu in time for her appointment. If anybody started snooping around, she was here simply for her postpartum check-up but her time with Dr Zungu, medicine and Lungelo had technically come to an end and the relationship they'd formed thanks to him had extended past patient and specialist.

Fezile listened intently to Mandisa's problem before giving her advice, the answer to which meant that she'd have to pull some strings of her own but Mandy would have to play her role and get a few key things in order to make this happen and get the help that she needed. DNA. From both men, she didn't know which was the less of two evils or how to go about it, either way, she knew she had one person willing to help. Calling up Nodumo she explained her dilemma and even before she'd confirmed things with "Mr I want us to give things another chance," Nodumo was ranting on how much of an ass Spha was as if she didn't get that vibe when they'd met with him the first time but with enough begging, she agreed to meet him and on their date get what was asked of her. That was part one done, it was down to part two, everything now rested on her shoulders, so much pressure until a phone call from Faith took it away.

"You've been one hard lady to get a hold of," she sighed.

"What a lovely surprise, I wasn't expecting this and shouldn't you be in school?"

"That's the whole point of a surprise, no? And who's to say I'm not? You and your assumptions though, where are you, we need to talk,"

"I'm busy, what's the matter? You sound distressed. Are you in trouble?"

"Yes, I am but-,"

"No, no. this is all you. You got me into this mess, you need to get me out, it's only fair, please, quickly hurry," she cried.

"Okay," Mandisa sighed as she took down the details of Faith's location before heading off to see the father of her children, to become yet another disappointment by not being able to stay. By being a trailer to the movie he was so excited to come see.

14

Some time and a few disappointments later

Sakhile had agreed to give Mandisa another chance. As much as he didn't condone the relationship between how the two families got along, the least he could do was have a dignified relationship, for his son's sake. The woman in question was an expert at sticking her nose in other people's business and should've been a journalist, not an accountant. Sakhile had second thoughts, with each intersection it forced the car to stop making them stronger given the last time their families met. Was it a possible set-up to finish him off now that they were out of jail? But Mandisa, hopefully, wasn't like her siblings.

As Mandisa waited for the infamous number plate, Dube-1-ZN, she came to the realisation or at the very least make and stand behind her own decisions and not those of others. When was the last time she knew what it felt like to be truly happy? What difference would an unhappy teenager make if it didn't get to live the life they'd envisioned? So what if she didn't want her family spoilt financially, all because it made her feel like a whore regardless of whether it made her one was a debate for another day? As she stood there on the pavement, waiting for an all too familiar Range Rover, a BMW, something. She was embraced by a Mercedes-Benz from the same family plate, Dube-5-ZN, a tiny two-seater with black windows, a tell-tale sign that it had gone through a lot of renovations with the massive alloy wheels accompanying it. She hesitantly entered and no sooner than when she did, set off an argument about Lungelo's whereabouts dampened by takeaways. It was the perfect opportunity for Mandisa to gather some much-needed DNA as she could find in an extremely clean car. With stomachs full from either party, the conversation changed from

Lungelo's whereabouts to how he was going to sprout. Money and God forbid, visitation.

Mandisa, along with the help of Doctor Zungu, and now the DNA she'd amassed from "both fathers," was now able to answer the question that was no different than a mosquito bite in the centre of her back. She was going to be satisfied in knowing once and for all, who was the father of her child. From the moment she handed them over to the moment she was told they'd be ready in three days' time, she'd have to endure the longest 72 hours of her entire life. Even when it ended, it was plagued with delays and problems and the thought that she'd never find out what she'd set out to do in the beginning, was starting to become a possibility. But as soon as she found herself seated at the doctor's table, surrounded by degrees, qualifications plastered on the wall and fancy art to accompany it her thoughts began to consume her, making her sweat for no reason only to be rescued by her physician apologising for keeping her waiting.

After a slew of small talk, the following words hit home, distinct and unforgettable, "There's good news and bad news,"

"Doesn't matter which you tell me first, you're still going to tell me both," Mandisa shrugged.

"Very well. The good news is... Sphamandla Dlamini is not the father,"

"What! But...I'm so confused, how?" she said, squeezing her hands. "And the bad news?" she asked, remembering that there was still those as well.

"Would you prefer I tell you or show you?"

"Show me," she replied after a brief moment.

"Very well," the doctor nodded, getting up from his seat and headed towards the door. After a brief while, he returned with a teenager a little younger than Faith behind him. "Mandisa, I'd like to introduce you to Zanele," pointing at the girl. "Zanele, this is Mandisa Baloyi or as you will know her from now on. Mom,"

Mandisa's conscience blew on the words as though she were trying to cool a cup of hot tea, finding it hard to process and blatantly ignoring the eyes that stared at her awaiting a response to what had been said to her. Running a hand through her hair, her fingers at the back of her neck seemed to bring life into her eyes as she could face the reality before her, staring down at her daughter for the first time before hearing her speak.

"Ma,"

Hearing those words gave her visible chills that crawled down her spine but there was nothing she could do.

"Zanele," she said, opening her arms wide and embracing her in a tight hug. With her daughter mushed between her chest, she ignored her crying and whatever residue her eyeliner or whatever make-up she wore left on her blouse. "What, how, where?" Mandy stuttered.

The doctor sat them down at his desk before disappearing.

"It all started when I asked my dad," she sighed.

Mandisa looked at her in confusion, clearly oblivious to this girl's father or else they wouldn't find themselves in this predicament. She barely had a child for a year, let alone 16

"When my dad's drunk, it's easy to ask him about things he usually won't talk about, and that's when he answered my questions about why I didn't have a mother. He was honest enough to tell me I was adopted, but when I wanted to pursue being reunited with my birth mother, it required a little more alcohol," she shrugged.

Mandisa stared as she continued to listen.

"Whether it was out of guilt or a genuine need to help, thanks to the hangover. He began to help and thank God we could find a doctor who understood my problem or else we wouldn't be here today,"

Mandisa turned to thank the mystery doctor, but he was gone. No matter, what was of importance was that she now knew the truth about what was happening in her life. Her state of confusion was no more. How she'd love to see the look on Given's face when she brought Zanele home. She turned back to her daughter and gave her a nod before they headed for the door and parted ways after exchanging contact details. Irrespective of the massive burden that had been on her shoulders when she'd entered this building, she left with it no more, making space for something even bigger for her to carry, whether it would be even heavier was a question only a matter of time could answer. Knowing she had a daughter was one thing, but being free from blackmail was another.

The weeks that followed weren't the most ideal but within them, Mandisa was able to do what she'd promised to do, even more now that she knew the truth. Ironically, when Nodumo heard the news, she was thrilled although it took a lot out of Mandy to get her to keep her mouth shut. She just was mentally and more importantly, emotionally prepared for what was about to happen once the truth came out and this was still over her baby boy who just like his name had a right to live freely without being dictated to which right he was and wasn't entitled to. It's behaviour like this that made her breathe a sigh of relief that she didn't tell her about Zanele even though being the only one to know about her came hard, chances were, when she came out it would come back to bite her... hard. But she would cross that bridge when she got there. Right now, however, her phone beeped with a ringtone she'd personalised for only one person. Her allowance was in and being the head of the household meant that her brothers and mothers would have to honour what now became one of her favourite lines from the bible.

"Honor your father and your mother so that you may live long in the land the Lord your God has given you,"

Kind of ironic how she was meant to be humble but it left her smiling like an emoji that the very same people who used to give her shit for having a child, signing an NDA for donating her eggs for whatever greater good they may serve out there in the world were now dependent on her for water, lights and their next meal. One part of her wanted to leave home and live on her own, free from all the judgment that came with living under her mother's roof, but another part couldn't bring herself to do it. After everything they'd done for her, how they stuck by her side even when nobody else would, provided a roof over her head and even went to jail for her. Yes, Given and Emmanuel ended up there of their own free will, but the foundation on which that stint in prison was built was on top of the woman that reflected off the glass before her. With all this running through her mind she felt like a pregnant teenager preparing herself to tell her parents she was pregnant. Nobody could help but one person even though she detested the thought, there was no other option if she really wanted to fix things, make things right... for everybody.

15

At home, Emmanuel was nowhere to be seen. Leaving all but one person to babysit their mother. Who inundated her with questions rather than saying thank you when informed of this alongside a token of essential groceries to accompany the bread and milk that was already in the house. Financially, she had everything under control and so did Given but he was nowhere to be seen. With her only commitment being to God and then Emmanuel and Lungelo and everybody else afterwards. Joyce would live with her favourite individuals with only an American rap star and their lavish life trying to compete with her best life.

Meanwhile...

While mental questions of what was right and wrong consumed Mandisa. The Baloyi brothers didn't have any doubt since they'd left home to where they'd found themselves now, wandering aimlessly throughout DCTB. When Asanda laid his eyes on them for the first time since they'd left jail, his heart damn near booked a suite in the afterlife. Whether it was heaven or hell was yet to be determined as Given approached him with the silence of a ghost, his brother not far behind sealing off the exits.

"It's been a while hasn't it Dube?" Given asked. "But not long enough for you to look like you've seen a ghost, stop being so dramatic,"

Asanda's eyes popped, his pupils tracking Given as he navigated his way through his furniture and around his table towards him.

"Hello would be nice," he smiled.

Asanda stared at him, lost for words as Given towered over him.

"Uh ah," pulling Asanda's laptop away from him. "We wouldn't want to do that now would we?" Shaking his finger. "There's no need for violence, it's a reunion for God's sake,"

Asanda closed his eyes and started praying, his prayer becoming even faster as a hand tightened around his neck.

"While you're at it, ask him why you sent us to jail in the first place. When he answers that, ask him, which is what I want to know? "Why we're paying for medical bills for a man who's sick when there's nothing wrong with you? All three of us can see that, no?"

No sooner had Given finished his words when Sakhile burst in, taking Emmanuel by surprise and leading to an exchange of words and a little more allowing Asanda to finally use his laptop over Given's head. Although it would be ruined, it was of material nature and things of material nature could easily be replaced but the feeling of smashing Given with a laptop over the head wouldn't, that would last forever, for both parties. The scuffle lasted until the visitors were escorted out by security who was nowhere to be seen until now. Although the Dube's weren't a bloody mess, the injuries left on them required a bit of explaining whenever they were seen in public especially given their public persona. Once everything had calmed down and his brother was finally willing to open up about what was going on when he was sure they'd finally put an end to their harassment. Watching the trauma on his brother's face was unhealthy especially since he was the one who'd convinced him to get rid of all the private security back when these thugs were back in prison and look where that decision ended up.

If Asanda was paranoid before he would give a new definition to what the word meant now but the worst was yet to come as he zoned out from listening to him rant on about how they could ever leave jail when he had everything planned out so perfectly. Paid the right amount for the judge and even a bigger fee for the warden to give them as much shit as humanly possible, in order to teach them a lesson for trying to mess with him. Any form of bribery was meant to go through him so he could match or pay more than it, his plan was foolproof so he couldn't understand how they stood before him, like shadows in the shade, it was humanly impossible.

"Sakhile!!"

"I know right," he mumbled.

Asanda ran his hands over his head in frustration before picking up the fragments of his laptop that were left behind.

"I have a solution but you won't like it,"

"I'm open to anything at this point," Asanda said clicking his tongue.

"Forgiveness,"

"What?" confused.

"I know how all of this happened but I need you to forgive me for keeping quiet for so long. I need you to understand that I didn't want to hurt you, I still don't but I now realise the longer I keep quiet the harder it is not to,"

"Okay,"

"I need you to promise,"

"I promise," he said with a hand over his heart.

"It was me,"

Silence. It consumed the office only to be broken by Sakhile coughing a handful of blood, nothing serious but his wounds that would still need some attention. He hesitated to tell his brother what he'd want to know if the roles were reversed.

"I didn't do it to spite or undermine you," he sighed. I'm going through a lot and I need their help. Unfortunately, I can't get it while they're behind bars,"

"What makes you think she still wants to be with you?" he asked after a long while.

"Because she's willing to give it another go,"

"And what makes you think that's not because of your controlling behaviour? Don't act like you don't know how forceful you can be.

I'm sure you showered the girl with money, with my money no less, promised her the world and now when you're unable to keep up to your promise making other promises you won't keep,"

"Asanda, it's nothing like that, it's-"

"I don't need to hear your sorry excuses, I've heard enough," Asanda said, raising his hand towards his brother's face. "It's good to know where your priorities lie. Bros before hoes doesn't exist and judging by how she comes before anything else, nor does God,"

"Don't give me that shit. Play that spiritual and holy shit outside those doors not here with me," Sakhile pointed behind him. "

Asanda raised his arms in defeat.

"Look, I thought you deserved the truth, that's all. As my brother, you deserve that much, so that in the event they come back, you're in the right frame of mind to challenge them. Use logic and not fear,"

"Who says I'm scared of them?"

"My apologies then," Sakhile nodded, before heading towards the door accompanying a phone that vibrated in his pocket.

"And where do you think you're going?"

"Out,"

"I've stood here like a lamp post and listened to your speech, the least you could do is give me the same decency or respect to listen to my reply,"

"Text me,"

And with that, Sakhile was gone. Leaving his brother in silence before the sound of tyres screeching on the tarmac were the last mutual sound between them. The sound of those tyres might have sounded dramatic as he left the church but so does a bullet when it leaves a gun. The two objects had a lot in common, chief among them being the speeds they cut through the air. Sakhile pulled up at the home of the very people he'd beat up and waited for their youngest sibling to emerge from their home, he didn't have to wait long before it happened and when it did, he disappeared with her,

Mandisa was shocked at how ravaged Sakile looked. She knew exactly what had happened but wanted it to come from his own mouth rather than assume it even though it wasn't an assumption but he refused to acknowledge it. Ignoring it as if his black eye didn't exist. Despite how much she pushed him, he ignored her and the matter as though she were mad. His physical appearance even made her forget the reason for getting into the car in the first place. But then she remembered as soon as his groans reminded her of her son after relieving himself.

"I have something to tell you,"

"What?" he grumbled.

"I just need you to help me with this whole NDA thing, I want to untie myself from it legally,"

Sakhile looked at her, confused.

"I know this seems out of the blue but before you throw a tantrum, it has got nothing to do with your brother. Yes, I know, I've just chosen to keep my nose out where it doesn't belong. That said, this is where it does," Mandisa breathed heavily, "This might be me overreacting, but it just came to light that I have a daughter I knew nothing about. A daughter as old if not older than your niece, Faith,"

Sakhile looked at her, surprised.

"My initial reaction as well, and this is why I've brought you here, because I know you will understand having a child of your own, with me. Why you still don't want to come out and own it is between you and your brother and why you fear him so much even though you wear the pants in that house," she said, playing with the leather in the car. "But if we turn our attention to me for a second I'm scared Sakhile, I'm scared... please don't give me that look. I'm scared because I only know of two children that biologically belong to me. I don't know what you did when I signed my ovaries away, but I never thought in my wildest imagination it would be this. And if it's possible for me to be searched for, chased down and then be found so easily what's stopping another or another or God knows how many other children there might be out there from finding me... or worse trying to kill me because they have the wrong idea of me as a mother, I-"

"Stop!" grabbing her by the shoulders. "Look at me. Take a deep breath, you got this and I'll be right here to go through it with you. I love you, if you don't believe me then let these bruises be physical proof of that."

Mandisa smiled at him

"As for your ovaries, I don't know what happened to them, they're as good as lotto numbers right now. But what I can tell you is that we'll cross that bridge when we get there. Also, if the only condition of being with you is for me to raise Lungelo in the light and not the shadows, then so be it, let him grow up with a father and spare you the job of being both. Let my brother's lies ruin his life, I now realise that money alone can't raise a family but that said, I'm going to need you to give me a little time to come out in the open with all of this as it wasn't easy coming out with it to you, to begin with, and I pray you understand,"

She nodded empathetically.

"So what happens now?"

"What do you mean what happens now, we put all of this into motion that's what,"

"Oh yeah, speaking of things in motion, whatever happened between you and the dude pretending to be the father of my child?" Sakhile asked.

"You... only now you concern yourself with my wellbeing, what's it to you anyways. What difference does it make?"

"None, I'd just like to know while I still can?"

"What do you mean while you still can?" Mandisa asked with her face contorted.

"As you said, and I quote... what's it to you anyway, what difference does it make?" he said with his hands raised beside him.

"WeSakhile," she growled.

"All I'm saying is not all expressions of love are expressed with chocolates and roses. Just cause I don't give you one doesn't mean I don't appreciate you,"

"You dirty son of a-" Mandisa was interrupted mid-sentence by her phone, a surprise phone call by none other than Doctor Zungu. What started off as a check-up from a nosy doctor trying to find out how things went only ended up in more confusion when they asked if she would be comfortable meeting another physician.

TBC

Don't miss out!

Visit the website below and you can sign up to receive emails whenever Londa Cele publishes a new book. There's no charge and no obligation.

https://books2read.com/r/B-A-XGKG-MKQJC

BOOKS 2 READ

Connecting independent readers to independent writers.

Also by Londa Cele

The Gifted
Someone New
Angels of Death

Unsupervised
Questionable Decisions

Standalone
Nomalungelo
Wedding Vows
Thando's Strength

Watch for more at www.londacelenovelz.wordpress.com.

About the Author

Londa Cele is the founder of LondaCeleNovels and the author of Nomalungelo & Wedding Vows. Graduate of SA Writer's College and Toastmaster's recipient, but a shy one at that. Londa currently resides in South Africa and is fluent in 5 languages.

Follow him on Twitter @Londa_Cele

Read more at www.londacelenovelz.wordpress.com.

48003CB00005B/1940